PUFFIN BOOKS

The Worst Witch All At Sea

Jill Murphy started putting books together (literally with a stapler) when she was six. Her *Worst Witch* series, the first of which was published in 1975, is hugely successful. She has also written and illustrated several award-winning picture books for younger children.

D0783194

Some other books by Jill Murphy

(Titles in reading order)

THE WORST WITCH
THE WORST WITCH STRIKES AGAIN
A BAD SPELL FOR THE WORST WITCH
THE WORST WITCH ALL AT SEA

THE WORST WITCH'S SPELLING BOOK
(with Rose Griffiths)

JILL MURPHY

THE WORST WITCH ALL AT SEA

PUFFIN BOOKS

PUFFIN BOOKS

Published by the Penguin Group
Penguin Books Ltd, 27 Wrights Lane, London W8 5TZ, England
Penguin Putnam Inc., 375 Hudson Street, New York, New York 10014, USA
Penguin Books Australia Ltd, Ringwood, Victoria, Australia
Penguin Books Canada Ltd, 10 Alcorn Avenue, Toronto, Ontario,
Canada M4V 3B2
Penguin Books (NZ) Ltd, Private Bag 102902, NSMC, Auckland,
New Zealand

On the World Wide Web at: www.penguin.com

Penguin Books Ltd, Registered Offices: Harmondsworth, Middlesex,
England

First published by Viking 1993
Published in Puffin Books 1994

Puffin Film and TV Tie-in edition first published 1999
4

Copyright © Jill Murphy, 1993
All rights reserved

The moral right of the author/illustrator has been asserted

Filmset in Baskerville

Made and printed in England by Clays Ltd, St Ives plc

Except in the United States of America, this book is sold subject
to the condition that it shall not, by way of trade or otherwise, be lent,
resold, hired out, or otherwise circulated without the publisher's prior
consent in any form of binding or cover other than
that in which it is published and without a similar condition including this
condition being imposed on the subsequent purchaser.

British Library Cataloguing in Publication Data
A CIP catalogue record for this book is available from the British Library

ISBN 0–141–30646–7

TO CHLOE AND ALICE WITH LOVE FOR EVER

CHAPTER ONE

A violent snowstorm greeted the pupils of Miss Cackle's Academy for Witches as they returned to school for the first day of the Summer Term.

There were two terms dividing the school year. The Winter Term, which began in September, continuing until January, and the Summer Term, which began in March, ending in July. With five solid months to each term, you can imagine how bleak it felt during the middle months, when every minute seemed like an hour, with no light flickering at the end of the tunnel.

The girls were used to appalling weather for the first few weeks of the Summer Term because it was so early in the year, but this time it had surpassed itself.

Miss Cackle, the kindly headmistress of the school, watched from her study window as the pupils arrived in ones and twos, battling to stay on their broomsticks, cloaks turned inside out and summer dresses flapping wildly in the screaming wind.

Mildred Hubble, a second year, already renowned as the worst witch in the school, lurched out of the yellow-grey clouds with a crust of snow covering her broomstick, cat, suitcase and summer dress, which was a new design this year.

Miss Hardbroom (Mildred's horrifically strict form-mistress) had decided that the old design of black and grey checks was too frivolous for the girls and had persuaded the headmistress to have them replaced with nice, sensible, plain black. Miss Cackle had meekly agreed with Miss Hardbroom's plan as she usually did (being a person who always avoided any trouble), but she had secretly rather liked the old uniform. The whole business had caused much merriment among the girls, who could scarcely believe that anyone, even Miss Hardbroom, could consider black and grey checks and grey ankle socks to be frivolous.

Mildred wondered if she was actually frozen on to her broomstick as she struggled to steer it over the wall and into the yard. She turned to check that her tabby cat was still with her, as the poor creature was terrified of flying at the best of times and had been yowling his head off for the whole journey. He was, but as they cleared the top of the gates by inches, the little cat attempted to jump off, causing Mildred to crash-land into a deep snowdrift which curved in an elegant arc against one of the broomstick sheds. It was quite sheltered in the yard and Mildred lay in the snow getting her breath back, watching the other pupils coming in to land, most of them more successfully than herself.

'You are a pain, T-T-Tabby,' said Mildred, her teeth chattering with cold. 'How am I ever going to get anywhere in this place while I'm st-t-tuck with a cat like you?'

Tabby shook himself, and snow sprayed over Mildred's already snow-covered face. She even had icicles hanging from the brim of her hat, and Tabby's fur stood out in little frozen peaks. They made a sorry pair.

'Maud, is that you?' Mildred called out, as a hunched bundle of broomstick and baggage wobbled over the wall and glided into the snow a few yards away.

'Millie!' yelled a voice which was unmistakably that of her best friend.

'Incredible weather, isn't it? And they call it *Summer* Term!'

Mildred scrambled to her feet, brushed off as much snow as she could and waded across to Maud, dragging her suitcase and broomstick behind her. Tabby had now assumed his usual position, draped around Mildred's shoulders like a fur stole.

'Do you think they might light a few fires as a special concession?' asked Mildred.

'I shouldn't think so,' said Maud. 'You know what they're like – healthy fresh air at all times. What about the uniform then? Frivolous! I ask you!'

The yard was rapidly filling up with pupils all stamping their feet to warm themselves and hoping that they might be allowed inside instead of assembling in the yard as usual. They made a rather dramatic sight dotted about like crows against the glaring white.

The main door opened and Ethel Hallow, a member of Mildred's class generally known for her bossiness, especially towards Mildred, appeared with a note which she pinned to the door.

The note read:

NO ONE is allowed inside without permission. Girls must assemble in lines in the yard. When the bell rings, they should proceed to the cloak-rooms in single file to deposit their bags and from there proceed to morning assembly in the Great Hall.

'I *told* you,' said Maud grimly. 'And how did Ethel get inside when we're all out here? That's what *I'd* like to know. Look at her, all dry and comfortable when everyone else is frozen stiff, waiting to be summoned out of the storm.'

'Watch out, Maud,' said Mildred. 'She's beckoning to us.'

'Mildred Hubble,' shouted Ethel from the shelter of the doorway, 'Miss Cackle wants to see you in her study straight away. Didn't take you long this time, did it?' She couldn't resist sneering. 'How many minutes have you been here – five, is it?'

She pulled a face and ducked inside, closing the door behind her.

'Oh, Maud,' said Mildred. 'Miss Cackle must have seen me crash-landing. You'd think she'd have let me off a bit, with a force nine gale and a blizzard going on.'

'Never mind, Mil,' comforted Maud. 'I wish she wanted to see *me*. There'll be a fire roaring in her study and at least you'll be able to warm up. Anyway, I'll bet it's not even about your crash-landing – probably something perfectly pleasant.'

'Perfectly pleasant!' giggled Mildred. 'Well, I'd better go and find out what I've done. Why don't you see if you can find Enid while I'm in there? She must have arrived by now.'

Enid was their other friend.

'Good idea,' said Maud. 'Best of luck then.'

Mildred gathered up her suitcase and broom and made her way up the snow-clad stone steps and in through the heavy front door.

CHAPTER TWO

It wasn't much warmer inside the school than out in the snow-swept yard. There was no glass in the castle-style windows, and there were little drifts of snow in regular heaps beneath the window-ledges all the way along the corridor. Miss Cackle's door loomed ahead and Mildred slowed to a snail's pace to put off the moment when she would have to enter and see what she had done now, ten minutes after the start of term.

She knocked very softly, hoping that she might not be heard.

'Come in!' called Miss Cackle's cheery voice from inside. Mildred pushed open the door and there was Miss Cackle sitting at her desk with a glorious log fire blazing in the grate.

'Ah, Mildred, my dear,' continued Miss Cackle. 'Come and sit here by the fire, you look absolutely frozen. I want to have a little chat with you. Ghastly weather, isn't it?'

'Yes, Miss Cackle,' agreed Mildred politely, feeling less anxious as she noted the good-humoured tone of Miss Cackle's voice. Perhaps it *was* something 'perfectly pleasant' after all, as Maud had said.

Mildred sat down gratefully in a chair next to the hearth and Tabby jumped down from her shoulders and curled up so near the grate that his fur almost caught fire.

'Tabby!' called Mildred, clicking her fingers. 'Come back here at once.'

But the little cat was too intent on thawing out to obey his mistress's orders. Also thawing out were the icicles on Mildred's hat and three of them descended simultaneously to the floor with a gentle clinking sound.

'Now then, Mildred,' said Miss Cackle, pressing her fingertips together and surveying Mildred over the top of them. 'I wanted to speak to you about that little cat of yours. Sweet, isn't he?'

'Oh yes, Miss Cackle,' said Mildred. 'He's *very* sweet. Not very *good*. I mean I can't get him to do anything right and he's still petrified of flying, but he's very good-natured and –'

'Yes, dear,' said Miss Cackle. 'I can see that he's a charming little cat, but I was watching your arrival just now and I couldn't help noticing that you were pulled off balance by the cat as you came over the gates. He really is a

rather useless creature, despite his nice nature and he *looks* terrible too when we're all on display – hanging on by his claws, spread out flat, when all the other cats are sitting up nice and straight by now – except for the first year's kittens, of course. Yours has never really got past the kitten phase, has he, my dear? And of course he has completely the wrong markings for the school and looks very untidy next to the black ones.'

Mildred stared at Miss Cackle, a wave of alarm spreading through her. Another icicle broke from her hat and fell into her lap.

'Anyway, dear,' Miss Cackle continued. 'I was wondering if a more normal, regulation black cat might possibly help you with your studies. One of the third-year girls, Fenella Feverfew, transferred to Miss Pentangle's Academy last term and left behind her extremely well-trained cat – they have owls at Miss Pentangle's, so she had no use for a cat. *You* could have it if you like.'

Mildred was appalled. She scooped Tabby from the hearth and clutched him to her damp, unfrivolous summer dress, the remaining icicles tinkling on to the floor as she did so.

'But what about Tabby, Miss Cackle!' she exclaimed. 'I mean, it's very kind of you to consider me like this, but I've had him now for nearly two years and he depends on me – especially as he isn't very clever, and I'm very fond of him.'

Miss Cackle smiled indulgently at Mildred, who looked rather appealing standing in a puddle of melted snow, her clothes and plaits dripping wet, with the pathetic little cat clasped to her heart.

'Now then, dear,' she said. 'There's nothing to worry about. Miss Tapioca, the school cook, was only telling me this morning that the kitchen is having a mouse problem and that she needs a good mouser. I would say that little Tabby here is just right for the job, wouldn't you? And it won't matter about his stripes, tucked away out of sight down in the kitchen.'

'But, Miss Cackle,' said Mildred, 'Tabby's frightened of mice. He doesn't —'

'Nonsense, Mildred,' laughed Miss Cackle. 'No cat is afraid of mice! What an idea. No, I think your work will improve no end if you accept my offer of Fenella's cat. And Tabby will have the time of his life down in the kitchen chasing mice all day and curling up by the range when he's tired. Off you go now. Miss Tapioca is expecting you — I rang her a moment ago. Run along, dear, or you'll be late for assembly. Miss Tapioca has Tabby's replacement in a basket downstairs.'

'Yes, Miss Cackle. Thank you, Miss Cackle,' said Mildred, trying unsuccessfully not to cry. She held Tabby even tighter and went out into the corridor, where the icy wind struck her in the face as she left the warm fireside behind her and closed the door.

CHAPTER THREE

The kitchen was in the basement of the school. It was reached by several long, dark corridors and narrow staircases. It took about half an hour to get there from the dining-hall, which

28

explained why the food was always stone cold.

'Now don't be scared, Tabby,' Mildred sobbed into the little cat's rumpled fur. 'I'll work out a plan to get you back with me again. I'll sneak down and give you extra training sessions so you'll get better at flying, and perhaps I could make you a little black coat to hide the stripes. I don't know why they're being so funny about that now, after all this time. *They* gave you to me in the first place. It's not fair.'

There was great activity in the kitchen, which, because of its gigantic range, was mercifully warm. Over the range bubbled huge cauldrons of the atrocious porridge to be served for the girls' breakfast, after assembly.

Mildred stood unnoticed in the doorway watching the four undercooks charging about. Miss Tapioca, a large person, proportioned very much like a cottage loaf, with white hair bundled into a hairnet, sat at one end of the fifteen-foot-long kitchen table looking up a recipe.

'Ah, Mildred Hubble!' she said, glancing up and seeing the bedraggled Mildred lurking in the shadows. 'Have you brought our new mouser? Come and show it to us, girl. Don't just stand there staring.'

Mildred brought Tabby out from beneath her cloak and held him up. The four undercooks had gathered round as well and they all tickled him on top of his head and smoothed his wind-blown fur.

'Just right for a mouser,' said Miss Tapioca. 'And here is Ebony in exchange. Much too intelligent and well trained to be wasted in the kitchen. Well, put the cat down, Mildred – unless you want to stay with him and catch mice yourself?'

She handed Mildred the basket. Mildred could see a pair of brilliant green eyes gazing at her from the shadow inside. Tabby, nicely warmed up by the hot kitchen, had retreated to his favourite position round Mildred's neck. There was nothing else to be done, except to take the basket and go.

'May I come and visit him?' asked Mildred, her voice quivering as she uncurled Tabby from her neck and placed him in Miss Tapioca's arms.

'I don't think that would be very sensible, Mildred,' said Miss Tapioca, holding Tabby in a very tight grip as the little cat was grimly trying to get back on to Mildred's shoulders. 'He will be much too busy chasing mice to spare any time for visitors. Off you go and take care of Ebony − now that really *is* a cat to be proud of. You'll forget this little scruff in five minutes once you've been out flying with a cat like Ebony. Listen! There's the bell for assembly. You'd better hurry.'

Mildred left the kitchen without looking back. She could hear Tabby yowling desperately as he tried to follow her. She dived up the stairs two at a time, ran to her room, dumped her suitcase, broomstick and the cat-basket and sprinted the last few corridors to join Maud and Enid marching into the Great Hall.

'Hello, Mil,' said Enid. 'What's wrong?'

'What's the matter, Mildred?' asked Maud. 'You look as if something ghastly's happened.'

'It has,' said Mildred, bursting into tears as quietly as possible, bearing in mind the fact that they were on their way into assembly. 'I'll tell you about it later.'

After assembly, during which Miss Cackle announced that lunch-break would be in the Great Hall instead of the yard because the snow was already several feet thick, the girls trooped off to their form-rooms, to be greeted by their form-mistresses.

Mildred's form were unfortunate enough to be presided over by Miss Hardbroom, the most terrifying mistress in the school. She was a genius at reducing her pupils to a gibbering heap with one withering glance. No one ever dreamed of passing a note, or giggling, or even speaking, unless asked a question, during Miss Hardbroom's lessons.

On the way to class, Mildred managed to tell Enid and Maud the sad news about Tabby.

Miss Hardbroom was sitting bolt upright behind her desk, waiting for the girls to settle, as they all filed into the room and took their places, arranging books and writing-equipment in their desks. The room was only fractionally warmer than outside, and the girls discreetly rubbed their feet and blew on their hands in a futile attempt to warm themselves up.

'Come along now, girls,' said Miss Hardbroom. 'Stop all this silly nonsense. It isn't *that* cold. Lunch-break isn't far away, and then you can all

36

run briskly around the Great Hall to get yourselves nice and warm. Anyway, girls, welcome back for the Summer Term – Mildred Hubble, what is the matter *now*?'

Mildred looked at her feet, embarrassed by the tears which she could not stop from rolling down her cheeks.

'It's her cat, Miss Hardbroom,' said Maud. 'Miss Cackle sent it to be a kitchen mouser, and Mildred's got Fenella Feverfew's, because Fenella left it behind when she left last term.'

'Well, Mildred,' said Miss Hardbroom, 'I don't know what you are
crying for. I would have seen it more
as a cause for celebration if I were
you. Fenella's cat is an absolute credit
to the school. I hope we shall soon see
a marked improvement in your flying,
without that nuisance of a tabby. Sit
down and pull yourself together at
once.'

'I have an announcement to make,
girls,' she continued, 'which should
cheer Mildred up considerably. Mr
Rowan-Webb, the magician Mildred
rescued from the school pond last
term, has written and asked if Mildred
and her form would like to spend a
week at his home by the sea during
the Summer Term, by way of a thank-
you to Mildred.'

There were gasps of delight from
the girls, who all turned to Mildred
with joyous comments.

'It seems that we all have *you* to thank for this little treat,' said Miss Hardbroom, making it sound as if Mildred had done something wrong.

Mildred didn't know whether to smile or look solemn.

'Goodness me, girl,' said Miss Hardbroom, noting Mildred's anxious face. 'Surely the thought of a week at the seaside is a cheering thought?'

'Oh yes, Miss Hardbroom,' sniffed Mildred, 'it's cheered me up very much. But I was wondering if I could bring Tabby with me as a little break from the kitchen. I wondered if it would . . .' Her voice trailed away as she saw Miss Hardbroom's eyebrow arch into a slant, like a poised spear.

There was no point in continuing. Mildred stared down at her feet and tried to look suitably pleased about the holiday, which was difficult when trying not to cry.

Maud sneaked a hand under Mildred's desk and squeezed her friend's arm. They both knew that a holiday would be no fun at all, with Tabby left behind in the kitchen wondering why Mildred didn't come to collect him.

CHAPTER FOUR

Gradually, the weather improved. It stopped snowing, the snow melted and soon the girls were all out in the chilly playground again, trying to devise new ways of keeping warm. The holiday was planned for the first week in May and everyone hoped that it might be warm enough by then to swim and have some fun. Mildred was the only one who didn't seem to be looking forward to the treat in any way.

'I wonder if there'll be a sandy beach,' said Maud, as they all stood ankle-deep in slush in the playground during lunch-break.

'– and caves!' said Enid.

'And a whole week of sunshine so that we can sunbathe and swim,' said Maud. 'What do *you* think, Mil?'

'Mildred *doesn't* think,' said Ethel Hallow, who just happened to be passing by on her way to the library. 'At least, I didn't see much evidence of any thought last term.'

'Oh, do leave me alone, Ethel,' said Mildred, hunching her cloak up around her ears.

'Not looking forward to our little treat then?' Ethel continued, in her usual sneering tone. 'I can't think why the whole thing's in honour of *you*, anyway. You're always messing everything up, you're the worst witch in the school –'

'Come on, Mildred,' said Maud, trying to keep the peace. 'Let's go somewhere else and leave Ethel to her sour grapes.'

They all trailed across the playground and tried to get out of the
wind by huddling in the broom-shed
(which is exactly the same as a bike-
shed, except that it houses broomsticks
instead of bicycles).

In fact, Ethel's observations about
the holiday in Mildred's honour were
very ill-advised. The whole incident

ending up with Mildred in the pond had been completely due to Ethel in the first place. During the Winter Term, Ethel had changed Mildred into a frog. Mildred had hopped off to find help and been discovered by Miss Hardbroom, who had put her into a jar in the potion laboratory. The frog-Mildred had escaped from her jar and fled to the pond to hide, where she had met the magician, Mr Rowan-Webb, also turned into a frog by enchantment. Mildred had rescued him and made sure he was reinstated as a human, so he was naturally very grateful to her, but Ethel was jealous of all the attention and praise which had been heaped on Mildred.

'What's up, Mil?' asked Maud. 'Aren't you even a *bit* thrilled about the holiday? Miss Hardbroom's already sent off for our regulation swimming-costumes and bathing-hats.

I think it's the most exciting thing that's happened for years.'

'Sorry to be a wet blanket, Maud,' said Mildred. 'I'm just a bit fed up at the moment, that's all.'

'Don't worry, Mil,' said Enid. 'I'm sure you'll be just as glad as everyone else by the time we actually set off to – where is it? What's the name of the place where the magician lives?'

'Gloom Castle, Grim Cove,' said Mildred.

'What a terrible name!' said Enid.

'You're joking!' exclaimed Maud.

'No I'm not,' said Mildred. 'I saw it at the top of the letter on Miss Hard-broom's desk. Sounds brilliant, doesn't it? I can just see us all frozen to death, doing broomstick practice up and down 500-foot sheer cliffs in our swimming-costumes – anyway, just imagine what the swimming-costumes will be like! If Miss Hardbroom thought our black and grey checked dresses were frivolous, goodness knows what she'll come up with for swimwear. Anyway, I'm bound to get everything wrong. Ethel's right really – I *do* mess everything up. I *am* the worst witch in the school.'

Maud and Enid felt awful. Mildred was truly down in the dumps, and nothing they could say seemed to cheer her up. What they didn't know was that she had another secret fear – like her embarrassing fear of the dark. Mildred couldn't swim. She had never learned how to, and even with arm-bands or a ring around her middle she was as terrified as Tabby on the back of the broomstick.

Tabby was the other problem. She missed Tabby so dreadfully that nothing could make her feel better – nothing except having Tabby back again – and she didn't know how to work out a plan to rescue him.

Ebony, Fenella's cat was a first-rate cat, almost as good as Ethel's. Mildred felt a twinge of disloyalty as she zoomed around the playground during broomstick practice with the perfectly trained Ebony bolt upright behind her. It really *was* a help to have a cat which was a credit to you. But at night, Ebony would set off through the window and along the school wall for a night of hunting, whereas dear, scruffy old Tabby had always spent the night curled up either on Mildred's chest or round the top of her head like a fur hat. Enid gave Mildred a rather nice furry tabby-cat hot-water bottle, but it only made her feel worse.

If only someone had invented a hot-water bottle that purred, thought Mildred sadly, as she curled up under the bedclothes in the dark.

CHAPTER FIVE

Every so often, Mildred made secret trips to the kitchen in an attempt to visit her abandoned pet. However, the kitchen was always bustling with cooks and dinner-ladies, and so far she had only caught one glimpse of Tabby, looking rather thin and even more moth-eaten than usual, curled up on top of a tall cupboard in a dark corner. Each time, someone had noticed Mildred skulking in the shadows, and shooed her away.

Meanwhile, the holiday at Grim Cove loomed nearer. One morning, Miss Hardbroom strode into the classroom with a large box containing the swimwear so eagerly awaited by Mildred's class.

Their spirits sank as Miss Hardbroom held up one of the costumes for their inspection. It was like one of those old-fashioned Victorian bathing-costumes, in black and grey stripes, with elbow-length sleeves and knee-length legs. The school badge, depicting a black cat on a yellow moon, was embroidered across the chest, and to crown this outfit was a close-fitting black swimming-hat.

Miss Hardbroom narrowed her eyes as her glance darted around the room.

'Well, girls,' she said coldly, 'I *had* hoped for slightly more enthusiasm from all of you. Miss Cackle has gone to considerable trouble and expense to kit you out with these superb garments. In fact, Miss Cackle has decided to join us for our exciting week on holiday. Isn't that wonderful? The remainder of the lesson will be spent making cards for Miss Cackle, to thank her for your marvellous swimming outfits.'

A faint groan of general disappointment rumbled around the classroom like distant thunder, as they all heaved open their desk-lids and rummaged around for their coloured pencils.

That evening, the members of Form Two all tried on their swimming-costumes in the wash-room before they got into their night-clothes. Mildred's

was slightly too large and rather baggy, and Maud's was unfortunately a little too tight, so that the school badge was stretched sideways across her front. Needless to say, Ethel's fitted like a glove and even managed to look quite smart.

'I have four cups for swimming from the first school I attended,' said Ethel. 'We had a huge swimming-pool there and I won cups for everything – diving, life-saving, relay racing and broomstick water-skiing.'

'Gosh,' said Mildred. 'What's broomstick water-skiing?'

'Don't you know *anything*, Mildred Hubble?' said Ethel in her infuriatingly superior tone. 'It's easy-peasy. You have skis on both feet, like ordinary skis, then you tie a piece of rope to the back of your broom, and off you zoom, holding on to the rope so the broomstick pulls you along like a boat. We can have races at Grim Cove. Of course, *I'll* win, but it's jolly good fun, even for all the losers.'

Mildred wondered if she ought to confess to Maud that she couldn't swim but it was so depressing constantly being hopeless at everything. She longed to say to everyone, 'Oh yes, I'm brilliant at such and such. Let me help you,' instead of spending her whole life desperately trying to memorize spells in the library and ending up in Miss Cackle's study explaining for the hundredth time why everything had gone wrong.

Also brewing in the back of Mildred's mind was a plan to kidnap (or catnap) Tabby from the kitchen and smuggle him away on the holiday with them. Even if she got into the most awful trouble on their return, she felt it would be worth it to spend a whole week with her much-loved pet, and she really did want to enjoy the holiday, particularly as it was a result of one thing that she had actually done right – saving Mr Rowan-Webb, the kindly old magician, from a lifetime of frog-dom.

'Are you *up* to something, Mil?' asked Enid one evening at dinner.

'Yes,' said Maud. 'You've got that far-away, vague sort of look you get when you're thinking up some scheme or other.'

'What?' asked Mildred vaguely, glancing up from a ghastly-looking plate of grey stew with a slab of yellow cabbage in the middle.

'I *told* you,' said Enid. 'She's *up* to something.'

'No I'm not,' said Mildred. 'And I'm really starting to look forward to the holiday now. I think we're all going to have a very exciting time.'

'Not too exciting, Mildred,' said

Maud uneasily. 'We don't want any trouble, do we?'

But Mildred wasn't listening. She was busily working out the finer details of her plan to snatch Tabby twenty minutes before take-off on their broomsticks for the flight to Grim Cove.

CHAPTER SIX

Luck was on Mildred's side for once. Miss Cackle announced that the journey to the magician's castle would begin at dawn. Each girl would have a packed breakfast to eat halfway through the journey, which would be ready and stowed away in their suitcase the night before. Miss Cackle also announced that, as it was a fairly long flight, lasting two hours, all pupils' cats would be transported in cat-baskets to save any accidents with sleepy or nervous cats falling off into the tree-tops below.

This meant that firstly the kitchen staff would not be up and about and secondly there would be a conveniently dark cat-basket in which to hide Tabby.

Mildred did consider telling Maud and Enid of her plan, but she knew that they would be so anxious on her behalf that it would only worry them, so she decided against it.

The morning of the holiday dawned. Mildred had been up and dressed for two hours, hoping that Ebony would be back early from his night out hunting, as he was sometimes out until long after dawn. Thankfully, on this occasion, he was back twenty minutes before the first blush of morning light stole across the cloudy, grey sky.

Mildred seized the elegant black creature as he positioned himself ready to spring from the window-ledge on to the top of the wardrobe. She bundled him into the cat-basket and crept out into the deserted corridor.

There was a dim night-lantern burning at the end of each corridor and at the head of each staircase, so she was easily able to make her way to the kitchen, once her eyes had adjusted to the gloomy light.

The kitchen looked strange with no one in it, all the pots and pans hanging on their hooks and no fires burning in the cooking ranges. The only sign of life was the pattering of dozens of tiny feet as mice swarmed all over the tables and worktops looking for left-over crumbs. Obviously Tabby was no use whatsoever in his new job.

'Tabby,' called Mildred softly. A shiver ran down her spine as she peered around into all the dark corners, huge creepy-looking cauldrons and storage cupboards with doors half-open as if someone might be lurking inside.

'Tab!' she called again. 'It's me. It's Mildred, I've come to fetch you.'

One of the cupboard doors creaked open and Mildred screamed, her heart banging in her ears with fright.

An answering 'Miaow!' set her mind at rest as Tabby came pattering softly to greet her, a half-eaten kipper dangling out of his mouth. The little cat was so delighted to see his mistress that he dropped the kipper and leaped into her arms, where there was much miaowing and cuddling, and even weeping from Mildred.

Tabby settled contentedly around Mildred's neck as if to say, 'Now where *have* you been all this time?' and Mildred bent down and unlatched the cat-basket.

Ebony stalked out looking rather annoyed at being shoved into the basket and then unceremoniously plonked out on to the cold, stone kitchen floor.

'Off you go, Eb,' whispered Mildred. 'I'm taking Tabby for a little holiday, so you can stand in for him while he's away. Oh, Tabby, they're all going to go *mad* when they find out. Perhaps they won't notice, with a bit of luck. Still *I* don't care. It's worth *anything* to have you back, even for a week. Come on, you'll have to go into the basket or we'll be found out before we even get there.'

Tabby didn't mind going into the basket at all. Mildred could hear him purring like a car-engine as she headed for the kitchen door. As she heaved it open, several mice skittered out from beneath the large table and dived past into the corridor, pursued by Ebony.

Mildred giggled, 'Oh, Tabby,' she said, scratching his head fondly through the wicker bars. 'You're such a hopeless case. I *have* missed you.'

CHAPTER SEVEN

peration Rescue-Tabby had taken longer than Mildred had calculated, and she arrived in the yard to find everyone, including Miss Cackle and Miss Hardbroom, all lined up and ready to set off. They were standing in rows, in absolute silence, as Mildred burst through the main door and clumped to her place in line.

'Ah, Mildred,' said Miss Hardbroom crisply. 'How kind of you to join us. Perhaps you had a little problem getting up so early in the morning?'

'Yes, Miss Hardbroom,' agreed Mildred, relieved to be provided with an excuse. 'And then I had to wait for Ebony to come in from his hunting and then I couldn't get him to go into the basket and *then* I couldn't . . .'

'That will do, Mildred!' snapped Miss Hardbroom. 'I really don't want to stand here all morning listening to a never-ending list of all the things you couldn't do before we were graced with your presence. Now then, if Miss Cackle is agreeable, we shall proceed to Grim Cove and the splendid holiday which awaits us.'

Miss Cackle smiled and nodded at the girls. 'Most certainly, Miss Hardbroom,' she said. 'Let us proceed at once! We don't want to waste one moment of our jolly holiday, do we, girls?'

Form Two let out a loud cheer of agreement.

'That is quite enough, girls!' exclaimed Miss Hardbroom. 'Miss Cackle doesn't want to be deafened. Now, Mildred Hubble, a word in your ear. Mr Rowan-Webb has kindly bestowed this holiday upon Form Two out of gratitude for your helpful action in saving him from the pond. He obviously thinks most highly of you, so let us hope that you will not do anything whatsoever to disillusion him. Do you think you can manage an entire week without drawing any unwanted attention to yourself? In other words, Mildred, no silly nonsense – all right?'

'Oh, definitely, Miss Hardbroom,' said Mildred, feeling distinctly nervous as she held the cat-basket containing the wrong cat underneath her cloak.

'Good,' said Miss Hardbroom. 'Then let us depart. Ethel, dear, lead on. Follow the river.'

The girls commanded their broomsticks to hover and hooked their suit-
cases and cat-baskets over the twigs at
the back. Then they all arranged themselves side-saddle, jammed their hats
on as firmly as possible and took hold
of their broomsticks – some more
grimly than others. Ethel sat as upright as a telegraph-pole, her fingers

70

loosely curled around the stick. At the other end of the scale, Mildred was hanging on so tightly that her knuckles were white and she was almost bent double.

Ethel led the class over the wall and down the mountain towards the shining river, which was like a mauve and pink ribbon in the sunrise.

'Gosh, Maud,' said Mildred. 'It looks really beautiful at this time of day, doesn't it? Perhaps we'll have wonderful weather and it *will* be a great holiday after all.'

'It won't be if your cat doesn't shut up,' said Maud, looking back at Mildred's cat-basket, from whence a desperate yowling had just started.

Ethel swooped back alongside Mildred. 'There's something *about* you, Mildred Hubble, isn't there?' she observed unpleasantly. 'I mean, even a superb cat like Ebony goes berserk the moment it falls into your clutches. Perhaps being worst at everything is catching – you know, like measles.'

She zoomed ahead again to take her place as leader of the Form.

Miss Hardbroom and Miss Cackle were in front of everyone and Mildred heard Ethel say, 'I just went to see if Mildred's cat was all right, Miss Hardbroom. Any cat of hers seems to become nervous of flying – even one like Ebony.'

'Thank you, Ethel,' said Miss Hardbroom. 'Most thoughtful of you, my dear . . . Mildred!' she called over her shoulder into the wind. 'What on earth is the matter with Ebony?'

Tabby was scrabbling at the basket and miaowing at the top of his voice.

'He ate rather a large mouse, Miss Hardbroom,' replied Mildred. 'I don't think he's feeling very well.'

'We'll take a look at him when we

land for our breakfast,' Miss Hardbroom called back.

Mildred was horrified. They had
not even arrived at Grim Cove and
she had already got herself into the
most awful trouble. One glimpse of
Tabby, and Miss Hardbroom would
probably expel her on the spot, holiday or no holiday.

CHAPTER EIGHT

After an hour of flying, everyone was beginning to feel exhausted and hungry. Although the sun had risen into a perfectly blue sky, the wind was cold so high up, and Tabby's desperate complaining was beginning to grate on everyone's nerves.

Miss Cackle and Miss Hardbroom signalled to the girls to begin their descent to an area where a loop of river passed through a wood with a large shingle bank on either side of the water.

'Breakfast at last!' whispered Maud to Mildred. 'I'm starving.'

Mildred wasn't listening. She was wondering how to get out of having Tabby examined by Miss Hard-broom.

'Land at the shingle bank!' called Miss Hardbroom, as they descended like a flock of birds into the woodland. 'Only a quarter of an hour for our break, girls. We must press on as soon as possible.'

Miss Cackle and Miss Hardbroom landed perfectly, followed by Ethel and the rest of Form Two, all except Mildred. Tabby finally stopped

yowling as he and Mildred fell off into
a dense thicket several yards from the
landing-place.

'I'm sorry, Miss Hardbroom,' Mildred's voice called apologetically from
the middle of the bushes. 'There's so
much on the back of my broom, I
think I must have put too much into
my suitcase. At least Tab . . . Ebony's
stopped making such a noise. He looks
much better now, what I can see of
him in the gloom. I seem to be a bit
stuck.'

'Shall I go and help her, Miss Hard-broom?' asked Maud.

'No, Maud,' said Miss Hardbroom wearily. She turned in the direction of Mildred's bush. 'Just stay where you are, Mildred. I think the sight of you would put me off my breakfast at this moment. We'll pull you out when we set off again.'

Mildred breathed a sigh of relief as she wedged herself into the branches of a rather prickly bush and rummaged in her suitcase for her package of sandwiches.

'It worked, Tab!' she whispered. 'They've forgotten about you. Now *please* calm down for the rest of the journey. I might break my neck if I have to make myself crash a second time! Look, Tab, they're tuna sandwiches, you can have some if you like. I don't think you'll be too keen on apple juice though.'

For a while there was no sound except the birds singing and the rustling of paper bags as the girls demolished their food. Somehow, whenever Miss Hardbroom was present, no one ever dared to speak, although they were allowed to chat during meal times provided the noise didn't get too loud.

'Ethel,' said Miss Hardbroom, as they tidied away the breakfast things, 'would you kindly assist Mildred in her plight among the bushes so that we may continue on our journey?'

Ethel bustled about self-importantly, attaching a rope to the back of her broomstick. Then she took off on the broom with a lasso of rope over her arm, rather like a cowboy, and called to Mildred to get ready.

Mildred arranged her suitcase and cat-basket over the back of the broom and caught the rope, while Ethel hovered overhead. In fact, Ethel dropped the rope on to Mildred's head so abruptly that it nearly knocked her out.

'Whoops!' said Ethel. 'Silly me! Are you ready, Mildred? One, two, three, UP!' And she sped off at forty miles per hour, while Mildred, plus broom and baggage, was jerked into the air flat out at the end of the rope, hanging on for dear life.

'Thank you, Ethel!' called Miss Cackle, who was watching with Miss Hardbroom. 'That will do, dear. Mildred is well clear of the bushes now.'

Fortunately, Tabby seemed less

hysterical for the second half of the journey. Perhaps he was exhausted, because he curled up in the gloomy basket and fell fast asleep, even though the wind whistled through the wicker-work and blew his fur the wrong way round.

CHAPTER NINE

ildred sat hunched on her broomstick feeling tired and anxious. She was beginning to feel that the Operation Rescue-Tabby plan had been a mistake. Even if no one noticed that firstly Tabby was missing from the kitchen and secondly Ebony had resumed residence, she wouldn't ever be able to let Tabby out at Gloom Castle or everyone would know. Perhaps she could just keep him in her room and only let him out at night when everyone was in bed, or if they had to share a room she could choose Maud and then let her in on the secret.

'There it is, girls!' Miss Cackle called out so suddenly that everyone jumped. 'There's the coast, and there's Gloom Castle. What a spectacular sight!'

The coastline was indeed a spectacular sight, though not exactly what the pupils of Form Two had hoped for.

For a start, the sun had disappeared

behind ink-black clouds and it was just beginning to rain. Then there was the coastline itself, which consisted of mile after mile of amazingly high and rugged cliffs meeting an angry-looking navy-blue sea amid a mass of jagged rocks and shadowy coves. The waves smashed against the cliffs, sending up clouds of spray so high that the convoy of pupils and teachers could taste the salt in the air.

'Look, Mildred,' said Maud, pointing to the castle, which was the only habitation in sight as far as they could see.

Gloom Castle looked even more forbidding than Miss Cackle's Academy. Delicate scarves of mist and sea-spray hung around its battlements. The windows were slit windows, like the Academy, but larger so that more wind could howl up and down the corridors, and seagulls perched screeching on every roof-top and window-ledge.

What seemed like several miles below was Grim Cove, with a tiny shingle and stone beach, a rather sinister-looking cave, a small boat at anchor and a large rock shaped like a cat's head about half a mile out to sea. There were hundreds of tiny steps cut

86

into the cliff-face leading down from the castle to the bay.

Mildred shuddered. 'No wonder they call it Grim Cove!' she muttered, as a squall of rain hit them like a water-cannon.

'Begin the descent, girls!' Miss Hardbroom's military voice whipped along the wind. 'Head for the inner courtyard.'

The descent was more difficult than normal, for various reasons. First of all it was difficult to see where they were going, with their cloaks tying themselves in knots and the blinding rain and wind in their faces, and secondly they did not know the layout of the castle and were attempting to land in a small enclosed courtyard inside the battlements.

To do this, they had to hover like helicopters and inch their way downward. Even Ethel found it heavy going, but eventually they all arrived in the rain-lashed courtyard, soaked to the skin and frozen stiff. Fortunately for Mildred nearly all the cats were yowling and screaming with rage, as the rain had driven in through their baskets and drenched them. No one gave Tabby a second thought.

The girls lined up in their usual rows trying to look as neat as possible under the circumstances, while Miss Hardbroom smoothed her hair and robes and Miss Cackle adjusted her hat.

Without any warning, the two carved wooden doors leading into the

yard burst open, and there was Mr Rowan-Webb standing at the top of the stone stairs smiling at them.

'Welcome! Welcome!' he said, waving a hand into the dark corridor behind him. 'What a foul day to make such a journey. Come in at once and get yourselves warm.'

He looked a lot better than when they

had last seen him, which was at Hallow-e'en, when Mildred had presented him to the Chief Magician, Mr Hellibore, and he had been changed from a frog to a human again. Then, his clothes were in rags, but now they were magnificent – a fine shade of emerald green with a bottle-green cloak and pointed hat. The cloak was beautifully embroidered all over with rainbow-coloured stars and moons.

Miss Cackle and Miss Hardbroom led the way up the steps into the castle and Form Two followed meekly behind, leaving wet footprints where they trooped along. The doors swung silently closed behind them, shutting out almost all the light except for a dim lantern hanging on the wall every few yards or so.

They made a curious sight, walking in single file with their broomsticks and bags hovering along behind them,

and the disgruntled cats miaowing
crossly from the depths of the baskets.
The dim lanterns threw huge shadows
up the walls as they passed by.

Mr Rowan-Webb led them into a huge stone hall very like the one at Miss Cackle's Academy only more sparsely furnished and much more draughty. There was a fireplace the size of an ice-cream van, but sadly no fire.

'Do sit down, ladies,' said Mr Rowan-Webb, indicating several faded sofas and chairs, most of them with the springs and stuffing hanging out. 'You must be worn out after all that flying.'

Miss Hardbroom turned to the

pupils, who were standing in a soggy huddle, unsure whether 'ladies' referred to them as well as Miss Hardbroom and their headmistress.

'You may sit down, girls,' said Miss Hardbroom. 'Tell your broomsticks to stand at ease.'

'So sorry about the weather,' apologized Mr Rowan-Webb. 'It's usually quite pleasant at this time of year. Anyway, there's a nice fire to warm you all up until I show you to your rooms.'

Everyone looked pointedly at the empty grate.

Mr Rowan-Webb looked too.

'Dear me!' he exclaimed. 'Do forgive me, ladies. I really am so absent-minded these days.'

He muttered the words of a spell, waved his arms at the fireplace, and with a *whoosh!* a glorious log fire appeared, banked several feet high and throwing out such a fierce heat that those nearest had to back away.

'Now then, where was I?' said Mr Rowan-Webb. 'Oh yes – rooms. I've given you three rooms in the west wing. One small room each for you, Miss Cackle, and you, Miss Hard-broom, and a large dormitory for all

the girls. The girls' dormitory only has camp-beds and cushions and sleeping-bags – rather a rag-bag of bedding, I'm afraid. There are only two proper guest rooms with brass bedsteads, and naturally those are for the teachers. Never mind, it's all fun on holiday, isn't it?'

'I shan't be here during the week,

though I shall come back on the last day. I'm still visiting various friends and relations whom I haven't seen for decades, since my awful incarceration in the Academy pond, and I promised Aunt Ethelburga a few days of my time.

'Now then, what else do I have to tell you – oh yes, there is a boat in the cove, but I think it's best not to take her out, as there are rather a lot of rocks round and about. Any questions before you set off to unpack your things?'

No one dared to speak.

'Come along now, girls,' said Miss Cackle cheerily. 'Don't be shy. There must be something you'd like to know.'

Enid put up her hand.

'I was wondering, Mr Rowan-Webb,' she said, 'if there are any legends or stories about caves or smugglers around the castle and cove.'

'There's only one tale *I've* ever heard,' said Mr Rowan-Webb. 'There's a strange rock shaped like a cat's head, out to sea directly in front of the cove. A local tale tells how a sailor was once shipwrecked and strug-

gled to the rock in raging seas, holding on to a chest full of gold and silver coins and jewellery. He crammed the chest into a crevice in the rock and swam to the shore when the sea had calmed. But when he went back by boat with friends to collect the chest, he couldn't find it. Legend says that it is still there somewhere on Cat's Head Rock. I must say it would be rather handy to find it, as the rock belongs to me and I could do with the money for a few repairs to the castle! It's so difficult to get to it by boat, what with the currents and rocks, that no one has ever really bothered to investigate, especially as it probably isn't a true story anyway. Any other questions?'

No one else spoke.

'Right,' said Mr Rowan-Webb. 'If you've all warmed up a bit, allow me to show you to your rooms.'

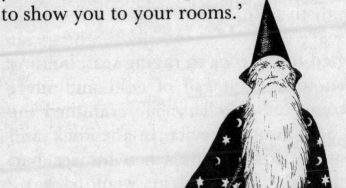

CHAPTER TEN

The dormitory was even more depressing than the castle and the coastline. Form Two stood and looked around in horror after they had been left to unpack.

There was a row of glassless windows at either end, which made the room like a wind-tunnel. Enough beds for all the pupils lined the other two walls, but they were, as the magician had said, a rather poor assembly of camp-beds, heaps of cushions, moth-eaten foam rubber and ancient cardboard-stiff blankets. The beds nearest to the windows were wet from the rain, which sprayed and dripped its way in.

Ethel dived for the only proper bed with a mattress, in the centre of one of the rows, and plonked her bags and broomstick on top.

'Bags I this one!' she announced. 'What a dump! Thanks for the holiday, Mildred Hubble. It's going to be a laugh a minute. At least the Academy will seem like a *real* holiday camp after a week in this place.'

Mildred didn't reply, as the entire Form was now scrambling for the best selection of beds.

'Come on, Mil!' called Enid, diving on to what looked like an old hospital trolley. 'There's a camp-bed next to mine with two blankets on!'

'No there isn't!' exclaimed Drusilla, a friend of Ethel, who barged Mildred out of the way and slammed her belongings on to the camp-bed with such force that it collapsed to the floor.

Mildred saw that the only place left was the worst one of all — a woven rush mat with a mildew-coloured sleeping-bag, laid directly underneath the window.

'Thanks for trying, Enid,' said Mildred, arranging her suitcase and broom against the wall and sitting down on the mat with the cat-basket hugged to her chest.

All the other members of Form Two

were busily letting out their cats for a stroll and a stretch and the room was suddenly full of black cats miaowing and entwining themselves round their owners' legs.

'Aren't you going to give Ebony some exercise?' asked Maud from her position four beds away, as she cuddled her own cat, Midnight.

Mildred shot to her feet.

'Er, I think I'm going to take him to Miss Hardbroom,' she said. 'Just in case he really *is* ill after making all that noise on the way here.'

And before anyone else could comment on the matter, she seized the basket and rushed out of the room.

Outside in the dark corridor, she stopped to contemplate what she was going to do with Tabby, now that they were all stuck in the same dormitory. If Ethel or Drusilla or anyone except Maud and Enid found out that she had defied the headmistress to bring Tabby, she would be in serious trouble.

As she stood and looked out of the window at the cove far below, she saw the boat bobbing up and down attached to a small breakwater, and a plan dawned in her mind like the thin shaft of sunlight which pierced the inky clouds above the castle.

'Come on, Tab,' she whispered. 'You're not going to like this one tiny bit, but it's the only solution.'

CHAPTER ELEVEN

Maud carried her cat across to Enid's trolley and sat down next to her friend. Enid looked up from sorting out piles of grey socks and underwear.

'Mildred's *up* to something,' said Maud darkly. 'I just know it.'

'Well, I wish she'd let *us* in on the secret,' said Enid crossly. 'She's been really strange for weeks – sort of vague and not quite with it.'

A shriek of laughter rang out from Ethel, who had overheard.

'*Do* forgive me for stating the obvious, Maud,' she said, 'but Mildred Hubble is *permanently* vague and not quite with it. If *I* were you, *I'd* start worrying if she was suddenly alert and getting A plus for everything!'

'Oh, do stop it, Ethel,' said Maud. 'No wonder Mildred gets in such a state with the likes of *you* hurling insults at her all the time. Anyway, you shouldn't be eavesdropping on other people's conversations. It's not right. Come on, Enid, let's move up to the other end so no one can hear us.'

If they had glanced out of the window at that moment, they would have seen Mildred, plus her cat-basket, making her way with great care down the cliff-face to the cove.

The rain had eased off to an unpleasant misty drizzle, which covered Mildred's clothes and hair in a fine net of droplets. The wind had suddenly abated, which made the descent far less terrifying than Mildred had expected, though the wooden handrail had rotted away in places and the steps were very slippery from the rain and sea-spray.

Although she was most relieved to arrive all in one piece on the pebbly beach below, the sight of the sinister breakers relentlessly pounding into sizzling foam as they clawed at the shingle made Mildred's heart begin to pound like the waves themselves.

Beyond the cove, which was actually quite sheltered from the wind by the height and shape of the cliff, the sea swelled alarmingly, as if a gigantic monster was breathing just beneath the surface and the strange Cat's Head Rock sat bang in the middle of the horizon with white crests appearing where the waves dashed against it.

'What a truly awful place, Tabby,' whispered Mildred into the wicker basket. 'I should have left you in the nice warm kitchen instead of bringing you here. I'm so sorry, little cat. What a mistress you're lumbered with – and to think that Miss Cackle thought *I* was stuck with *you*.'

First of all, Mildred examined the cave in the hope that it might be full of nice dry ledges and crannies, but it was unfortunately very shallow, more like a wind-blown sentry-box, with not one projection in the rock to hide a cat-basket. The boat was the only other hope.

Mildred opened the basket and let Tabby out for a run. Tabby looked most unimpressed by the sight of so much water, and stalked off to examine the cave, leaving Mildred to edge along the breakwater so that she could take a good look at the boat.

It was bigger than it had looked from Gloom Castle. There were two benches for rowers to sit on and at one end was a little cabin with a tiny door and window. A pair of oars was neatly lashed to the inside of the boat and there was a lifebelt on the side of the cabin, which made Mildred feel a little less panic-stricken.

Very carefully, Mildred lowered herself into the boat, which rolled alarmingly until she had found her balance, opened the door into the cabin and squeezed herself inside.

It was surprisingly snug. The rhythmic movement of the waves and the muffled slapping of the water even felt quite soothing after all the howling wind and rain. It really did seem the perfect place to hide a striped cat who shouldn't have come on holiday in the first place.

CHAPTER TWELVE

W here's Ebony, Mil?' asked
Maud, as Mildred arrived
back in the dormitory car-
rying the cat-basket with
the door open. 'He's all right, isn't he?'

'I don't know,' said Mildred. 'He
jumped out when I was on my way to
Miss Hardbroom, and disappeared out
of the nearest window along the battlements. I expect he'll be back soon.
He's a more adventurous cat than
Tabby.'

At least *that* part's true! she thought

miserably, feeling terrible at telling such an appalling amount of lies to her best friend.

'*I* think Miss Cackle should have let you keep that moth-eaten stripy rug,' jeered Ethel, whose clothes were now all folded into regimented piles on top of her suitcase at the end of her bed.

'No wonder poor old Ebony's made a bolt for it!'

Mildred had been working very hard on her spells and could now remember word-perfect the spells to change people into pigs, snails, frogs and centipedes, plus the antidote spells to change them back. She was sorely tempted to lash out and turn Ethel into a centipede for ten minutes, but managed to restrain herself when she remembered the other occasion, in her first term, when she had got into the most awful trouble with Miss Hardbroom for changing Ethel into a pig.

Just at that moment, as if to remind Mildred that it wouldn't have been a good idea at all, Miss Hardbroom materialized in the middle of the room.

'Excellent, Ethel,' she said, a wave of her bony hand indicating Ethel's neat pile of belongings. 'If only you all had such organized brains as Ethel

Hallow, Form Two. Ethel could make a rubbish tip look like an army barracks – even her cat knows how to arrange itself with taste.'

Ethel's cat, Night Star, was sitting bolt upright with his head slightly bowed on top of a pile of cardigans, looking like a statue from a museum.

'Yuk!' whispered Mildred to Maud. 'Doesn't she make you feel sick?'

'I do hope you aren't referring to *me*, Mildred Hubble?' said Miss Hardbroom icily.

'Oh no, Miss Hardbroom,' said Mildred, blushing.

'Then who *were* you referring to, Mildred?' asked Miss Hardbroom.

'Ethel Hallow, Miss Hardbroom,' muttered Mildred.

'Envy of Ethel's superior qualities will get you absolutely nowhere, Mildred Hubble,' snapped Miss Hardbroom. 'Apologize to Ethel, please.'

'Sorry, Ethel,' mumbled Mildred.

'That's all right, Mildred,' Ethel said, smiling sweetly. 'We all know you can't help it.'

'Now then, girls,' said Miss Hardbroom. 'The rest of the day is yours to study and rest after the long flight. Then we will have an early bedtime and hope that the weather is a little less bracing tomorrow so that we can play some games and sports on the beach.'

Having said this, she vanished.

Everyone stood around, looking nervous. No one dared to speak for several minutes, as they were never sure if she was still there or not.

Ethel was the first to speak, saying, just to be on the safe side, 'Well, I'm going to sit on my bed and brush up on my chanting. We've got a test during the week, holiday or not.'

'Good girl, Ethel,' Miss Hardbroom's approving tones wafted
through the room making everyone
jump.

There was a hasty scramble as the
pupils of Form Two all dived for their
beds and took out their spell and chanting books and arranged themselves in
as studious-looking positions as possible.

After a while, everyone relaxed and began chatting again.

'What will you do if Ebony doesn't come back?' Enid called across the other beds to Mildred.

'Oh, he'll be back,' said Mildred vaguely. 'And even if he's gone for a few days, I'm sure he'll be back in time to go home.'

CHAPTER THIRTEEN

When Mildred woke up the next morning she had a stiff neck from sleeping beneath the window. She sat up to peer out through the mist and saw a watery sun lurking behind the clouds.

Her first thought was for Tabby, and she crept out of her sleeping-bag and clambered into her sports-kit of grey aertex shirt, knee-length black shorts, grey socks and black plimsolls. (Miss Hardbroom and Miss Cackle had decreed that everyone was allowed to wear sports clothes for the entire holiday.) As it was still very early and rather cold, she wrapped her cloak around her shoulders and tiptoed out of the dormitory.

Seagulls screamed and wheeled

around her as she picked her way carefully down the rickety steps to the cove. To Mildred's delight, the sun had burnt through the clouds and the mist rolled back across the sea, as if an invisible hand was rolling up a carpet before her very eyes, and there below her lay the sea, sparkling and calm, the boat gently bobbing like a bathtoy at the end of the breakwater.

Mildred's spirits lifted like the mist as the sun warmed her tousled morning hair, and she watched the sea turn bluer by the minute. It seemed a completely different place from yesterday.

Tabby was curled up on a pile of rope inside the shelter at the end of the boat. Mildred could see him as she peeped in through the window.

'Good morning, Tab!' she said, opening the door. 'I've brought your breakfast.'

Tabby sprang on to her shoulder with one bound and rubbed his head against her neck. He certainly seemed none the worse for his night on board the boat.

Mildred unwrapped the little parcel of food which she had brought. She had saved three fish fingers and a lump of soggy mashed potato from dinner the night before. In fact, it was nearly *all* the dinner, as they had only had five fish fingers to start with, as well as baked beans, but she knew Tabby didn't like baked beans, so she had gratefully eaten those herself. She had also brought some milk mixed with water, in a plastic bottle she had saved from their breakfast on the flight to the Castle.

Mildred went and sat on the shingle beach and watched Tabby exploring the seaweed.

'I'd better get back, Tab,' said Mildred after a while. 'They'll all come to investigate if they know I'm down here so early. I'll leave the window open a bit, so you don't get too hot. At least there's a nice breeze on the sea. I'll come back this evening and let you out again. Don't you worry now.'

Tabby wasn't at all keen about going back into the cabin. Mildred had to rugby-tackle him and stuff him protesting back inside.

Everyone was up and in the middle of dressing when Mildred arrived back in the dormitory.

'Well, fancy that,' said Ethel. 'Mildred Hubble the early riser. Been practising your broomstick water-skiing have you?'

'Something like that,' muttered Mildred.

'What a terrific morning!' exclaimed Maud, smiling joyfully as she looked out of the window. 'Miss Hardbroom just came in and announced that we're to spend the whole day on the beach! We've all got our swimming-costumes on under our PE clothes, Mil. You'd better get yours on too – oh, and don't forget to bring your swimming-hat and your broomstick. The magician's arranged for us to have breakfast on the beach as a special treat!'

Not too near the boat, I hope! thought Mildred, anxious that someone might hear or see Tabby.

Miss Cackle and Miss Hardbroom were waiting for the members of Form Two in the little courtyard.

'Good morning, girls,' said Miss Cackle, beaming. 'Such glorious weather, after yesterday.'

'I hope you're all very grateful to be here having this wonderful holiday,' snarled Miss Hardbroom, making them all feel guilty as usual.

'Yes, Miss Hardbroom,' chorused the girls.

'Yes, yes, Miss Hardbroom,' said Miss Cackle. 'I'm sure we're *all* delighted to be here. Now then, as we all have our broomsticks with us, we may

as well fly down to the cove instead of
using those rather worn-looking steps.
Mr Rowan-Webb has left a veritable
feast of a breakfast on the beach, so
the sooner we get down there the
better, *I* say! Take it easy on the way
down – the cliffs are very steep. I
think we should hover our way down
rather than attempting a nosedive.'

CHAPTER FOURTEEN

Breakfast consisted of the most delicious array of food. The girls were dumbfounded at the amount of choice. In fact, there was usually no choice at all, just grey porridge looking like half-set concrete.

'Don't just stand there gawping,

Form Two,' said Miss Hardbroom. 'Take a plate and anything you require. Anyone would think you'd never *seen* food before.'

The feast was spread out on two long trestle-tables. There were several jugs of orange juice, two silver dishes full of kippers (Mildred made a mental note that she must get one or two for Tabby), ten silver racks stuffed with toast, pots of butter, four huge jars of marmalade, two pots of Marmite, three silver dishes full of crispy bacon, a large dish of grilled tomatoes and two more loaves in case anyone was still hungry.

There was also a large pottery urn full of Cornflakes and two pottery jugs full of milk, plus several bowls of sugar. The bowls and plates were all a beautiful shade of midnight blue with tiny gold stars on them. The girls still didn't quite dare to help themselves.

'Tuck in, girls!' announced Miss Cackle. '*I'm* certainly not going to wait a moment longer!'

This was the signal they all needed and soon there was a noisy bustle of spoons and bowls being grabbed and everyone was piling up as much food as they could cram on to their plates.

'Steady on, Mil!' said Maud, as she noticed Mildred attempting to hide three kippers underneath two strategically placed pieces of toast.

'I'm *starving* this morning,' said Mildred. 'It must be the sea air!'

She had a plastic bag in the pocket of her voluminous shorts, and managed to slide in all three kippers with the minimum of mess while no one was looking.

After the girls had eaten everything in sight and were lolling around feeling so full that they could hardly breathe, Miss Cackle clapped her hands and chanted the words of a spell no one had heard before. At once the trestle-tables took off like a pair of giant seagulls and flew back up the cliff, where they disappeared out of sight into the castle.

'Mr Rowan-Webb lent me that spell, girls,' said Miss Cackle, 'as part of our breakfast treat – no washing-up for anyone this morning!'

Form Two cheered loudly.

'Now then, girls!' announced Miss Hardbroom. 'First of all, a word of warning. When your broomsticks are near the water their magic powers are far less efficient. That is to say, they don't work so brilliantly when their magic is damp. Of course in *some* people's cases, they don't work too brilliantly even in ninety degrees of heat.' Here she shot a glance at Mildred, who dropped her eyes to the beach, feeling aware of the illicit kippers congealing in her pocket. 'For this reason,' Miss Hardbroom went on, 'you will find it difficult to keep your broomsticks stable directly above the water. However, if the broomsticks are hovering a good few feet above the waves, they will be strong enough to pull you along behind on water-skis. Miss Cackle and I have stored the school skis in a crate in the cave, which you will see behind us. There are enough pairs to fit every girl, plus one piece of rope each. Please go and collect these items and come back to me.'

Thank goodness I didn't hide Tabby in the cave, thought Mildred, as she joined the scrum of pupils grabbing their equipment.

'This should be fun!' exclaimed Enid, emerging laden from the cave just as Mildred was going in.

'Has anyone tried broomstick water-skiing before?' asked Miss Hardbroom once the girls had lined up on the beach with all their gear.

'I don't mean to boast, Miss Hardbroom,' simpered Ethel, 'but I was champion at my junior school.'

'Excellent, my dear!' enthused Miss Hardbroom. 'Then perhaps you could show your fellow pupils what is required.'

Ethel set about fixing the length of rope on to the back of the broomstick. There was enough spare to leave several feet of rope, which she tied into a handle at the other end.

'Shall I give a demonstration, Miss Hardbroom?' asked Ethel.

'Thank you, Ethel,' said Miss Hardbroom. 'That would be most kind.'

Ethel took off her sports clothes to reveal her striped bathing-costume. She bundled her hair into the black bathing-hat and carried her broom-stick and the skis to the shallow water at the edge of the beach.

'Hover!' she commanded her broom, which remained lifeless in her hands. 'Miss Hardbroom — it won't hover!' Ethel was close to tears. 'This has never happened before, Miss Hard-broom — Miss Cackle, I'm so sorry!'

'Don't worry, Ethel!' called Miss Hardbroom. 'You've probably forgotten that it's a little too close to the water. Hold it above your head, dear.'

Ethel laughed to hide her mistake. She held the broomstick as high above her head as possible while standing on tiptoe.

'Hover!' she commanded. This time the broomstick was perfectly happy to remain in mid-air. 'Stay!' Ethel brandished a finger at the disobedient broom.

Then she sat in the water, pulled on her skis, and hunched up so that her shoulders were under the water. She held on to the handle at the end of the rope. 'Off you go!' she called.

The broomstick shot off like a rocket.

Ethel rose out of the water, perfectly balanced on the skis and roared away, skimming the water in a cloud of spray. She executed a figure of eight, almost touching the water as she leaned into the curves, then came back to the beach in a straight line, sinking gracefully into the waves at the edge of the shingle as she arrived.

'Stay!' she called to the broomstick, which screeched to a halt at once and remained hovering patiently in mid-air, with the rope dangling into the sea.

'Was that all right, Miss Hard-broom?' asked Ethel earnestly.

'Superb, Ethel!' replied Miss Hard-broom. 'Quite simply, superb. Now then, Form Two, let's see if you can all raise yourselves to Ethel's standard by the end of the week. Of course, I realize that it is *unlikely*, but you can at least *try*. I will be joining you for a spin later in the morning. Will you be joining us, Miss Cackle?'

Miss Cackle looked appalled.

'Er! Oh no, I don't think so, Miss Hardbroom!' she answered, looking embarrassed. 'I'll be going in for a quick dip though – if the weather stays pleasant!'

The girls exchanged delighted glances as they imagined Miss Cackle in a swimming-costume.

'The sea-level will probably go up several feet if Miss Cackle goes swimming!' giggled Mildred.

'What was that, Mildred?' asked Miss Hardbroom.

'Um – I was just discussing the er – the laws of *science*!' replied Mildred. 'You know: when you put stones in a jar of water and the water-level goes up. I was wondering if – you know – with all this sea-water around we could try a little experiment later on, to see if –'

'I'm glad to note that you are suddenly so fascinated with the laws of science, Mildred,' said Miss Hardbroom. 'I must set you a little test to occupy your inquiring mind in case you get bored on the holiday.'

'Thank you, Miss Hardbroom,' said Mildred.

Maud and Enid prodded their friend as they all suppressed a major fit of the giggles.

CHAPTER FIFTEEN

uch to Mildred's surprise, the rest of the day was extremely enjoyable. Even Miss Hardbroom seemed relaxed and almost friendly as the sun beat down on the sheltered beach and the waves danced on the shingle.

Much to Form Two's delight, Miss Cackle emerged from the cave, which she had been using as a private dressing-room, wearing an extremely tight knee-length bathing-costume made of black and grey spotted material, which showed every bulge. She was also wearing a frilly black bathing-hat made of drooping rubber petals, like a giant chrysanthemum.

'Super day for a dip, girls!' she called as she picked her way painfully through the pebbles and plunged into the sea, sending up a cloud of spray like a big dipper crashing through the water trough.

'This is the life, eh, Mil?' said Maud as she floated past Mildred, who was hopping along on one foot, making swimming motions with her hands in the hope that no one would notice her deficiency in the swimming department. 'Even Miss Hardbroom's having a sneaky sunbathe – look.'

Mildred screwed up her eyes against

the glare. Sure enough, Miss Hardbroom, though still demurely clad in a
calf-length black dress, was sitting leaning against a rock with her legs
stretched out in the sun and no shoes
or stockings!

'Cor, look at that!' said Enid. 'No
stockings! Whatever next!'

Miss Hardbroom stood up at that
point and looked out to where the
three girls were standing. They all
jumped and turned away.

'Come on!' said Maud. 'Start swimming again. She probably heard every word.'

'She certainly did, Maud Spellbody,' hissed Miss Hardbroom's voice from behind them. 'So you'd better be careful what you say.'

The three friends spun round and there was Miss Hardbroom doing an elegant crawl behind them. She was now wearing a close-fitting mauve bathing-hat and a black knee- and

elbow-length swim-suit with a purple
V set into the front. The whole transfor-
mation had taken place within the
space of half a minute.

After Miss Hardbroom had joined
them, no one felt inclined to splash
about or have any more fun, and everyone was soon grimly swimming up and
down in silent rows before sedately
getting out and sitting on the beach,
wrapped in their towels.

As the evening approached, Mildred didn't have a chance to sneak the kippers across to Tabby, with the boat in full view of everyone. In fact, it was rather embarrassing, as the kippers were beginning to smell awful after a day of being crammed into Mildred's shorts.

Mildred tried to hang back as everyone settled on to their broomsticks and began flying back to the castle in ones and twos. Unfortunately, Enid and Maud waited loyally as their friend took ages rolling up her swimming-costume in a towel, then purposely dropping it and rolling it up again and retying her plimsolls three times in a desperate attempt to be the last one left on the beach.

'Come on, Mil!' said Maud. 'We're having dinner as soon as we get back. Everything'll have gone by the time you get your laces perfect.'

There was nothing for it but to go back to the castle, kippers and all, and return later when no one was looking. At least she could sneak some more food and perhaps some milk for Tabby.

CHAPTER SIXTEEN

An opportunity presented itself at dusk, as Form Two were having an hour of leisure before going to bed. Maud was darning a hole in the toe of a sock and Enid was reading a manual on broomstick water-skiing, while the rest of the girls were bustling about, similarly employed. No one seemed to notice as Mildred slunk out of the door and made her way to the cliff steps.

She was halfway down when, to her horror, a voice called out from behind, making her jump out of her skin. It was Ethel.

'Hey, Mildred,' she called. 'Mind if I join you?'

'Er – no,' said Mildred. 'Of course not.'

'Where are you off to then?' asked Ethel with an unpleasant smile. 'It's a

bit ·dangerous on these steps, so I thought you might need some assistance with whatever it is. You know how clumsy you are!'

Ethel managed to say all this in a light, sincere tone of voice. If you hadn't known her, you would have thought she was genuinely concerned, instead of nosily trying to find out something secret.

'I was just going for a stroll on the beach,' Mildred improvised. 'I've got a bit of a headache, that's all.'

'Then why didn't you go to Miss Hardbroom?' asked Ethel. 'She'd have given you an aspirin or something. No, I think you're *up* to something Mildred Hubble and I'm going to get Miss Hardbroom and tell her, before it's too late and you get us *all* into trouble.'

They had reached the bottom of the steps by this time.

'Look, Ethel,' said Mildred. 'If I tell you, will you *promise* not to let on? Even Maud and Enid don't know.'

Ethel considered the matter. She felt

quite pleased at being let in on a secret which even Mildred's best friends didn't know about.

'All right,' she said. 'I promise.'

'OK . . .' said Mildred, racking her brains for a good story. 'You remember the story about the treasure out on Cat's Head Rock? Well, I was going to go out there, on the boat, and have a little look around to see if I could find it. It's a nice calm evening and it seemed a good idea. I thought the magician would be really pleased to have the treasure to buy things for the castle. I wasn't going to go *now*, maybe a bit later when everyone's asleep. I was just going to have a look to see if the boat's seaworthy.'

Ethel stared at Mildred.

'Well, *I* think it's a dreadful idea,' she said. 'The magician *told* us not to use the boat, and you'd probably wreck it or something – anyway, there probably isn't any treasure at all. I say, Mildred, you do smell *awful*. Don't you think it would be more to the point if you went back to the castle and had a bath? You smell like a crate of rotting fish.'

'Actually,' said Mildred, 'I sat on a kipper this morning and haven't had time to wash my clothes. Perhaps you're right about the plan to get the treasure. I think I'll go back to the dorm and forget all about it.'

They set off on the long climb back up the steps, Ethel leading the way. While Ethel's back was turned, Mildred took the kippers from her pocket and lobbed them on to the deck of the boat, meaning to come back after dark and give them to Tabby in the shelter. The window was just too narrow for him to squeeze out, though Mildred had seen him looking out during the day. Amazingly, no one else had noticed, and any mewing had been drowned by the sound of the waves and seagulls and the shouts of the girls.

Miss Hardbroom looked out of her window at the perfect evening sky and decided to take a broomstick ride. She rarely felt quite so pleased with life as she did today. For some reason, the warm weather and the delights of sea-bathing had made her feel completely relaxed. Even the girls did not irritate her quite as much as usual – except for Mildred Hubble of course. Mildred would have irritated Miss Hardbroom whatever the weather was like. There was something about the girl that just *got* to Miss Hardbroom, like a scratchy label sewn into the neck of a dress. It even annoyed Miss Hardbroom that they were only invited on the holiday in the first place because of Mildred's action in saving Mr Rowan-Webb from the pond. However, putting all irritation aside, Miss Hardbroom swirled her cape around her shoulders, commanded her broom to hover outside the window, and the cat, which was a particularly beautiful, smooth, black one with olive-green eyes, named Morgana, to sit on the end, and lowered herself on to it gracefully.

'Away!' she commanded. 'To the cave.'

Mildred and Ethel had just reached the top of the steps and they both ducked as Miss Hardbroom zoomed over their heads, rather like one of those low-flying fighter planes that sometimes appear from nowhere when you're out walking in the country. Miss Hardbroom did not see the two girls as she nosedived down the cliff-face and pulled up to a perfect landing next to the breakwater where the boat was tied.

A chilly breeze was coming from the sea and Miss Hardbroom wrapped her cloak around her as she put the broomstick into the cave to keep it from getting wet.

At once, Morgana sprang purposefully on to the breakwater and ran along to the boat. She had smelt the kippers and couldn't wait to investigate. Miss Hardbroom was intrigued to see the cat disappear into the boat. She was even more intrigued when she heard a desperate yowling and saw the scruffy-looking Tabby madly trying to squeeze himself out of the few inches of open window in the shelter. Poor Tabby was frantic with hunger and the sight of Morgana eating his evening meal was too much to bear.

Miss Hardbroom climbed aboard the boat to investigate. She recognized Tabby immediately, and her eyebrows knitted together like storm-clouds as she made her way through the boat to the shelter. A slight breeze had come up and the boat was bobbing and swaying, making it difficult to keep her balance. Miss Hardbroom had forgotten her own cat, now crouched underneath one of the benches wolfing down the kippers as fast as possible.

The boat lurched and Miss Hardbroom unfortunately braced her foot on an unexpected piece of fish skin, which zipped her over backwards, banging her head on the seat as she fell. A shower of stars and exploding lights cascaded past her eyes as she lost consciousness. Then there was no sound, except for Tabby's pitiful mewing, Morgana's munching and the sea slapping at the sides of the boat.

CHAPTER SEVENTEEN

Of course, Ethel hadn't be-lieved Mildred when she said that she had given up her plan to visit the rock. She felt quite sure that Mildred would go back again, perhaps after dark. Mildred was such a bad liar and schemer, that she always gave herself away. Ethel could tell, by the way Mildred kept glancing out of the window and wandering up and down the dormi-tory. Even Maud and Enid had no-ticed something was wrong.

'What's the matter, Mil?' asked Maud. 'You look so jumpy all the time.'

'Nothing!' exclaimed Mildred in a falsely bright voice. 'Nothing at all!'

Ethel smiled secretly to herself. She had been a little worried in case Mildred actually did manage to take the boat to Cat's Head Rock and find the treasure. The thought of everyone praising Mildred's cleverness was just too upsetting for words. Of course, it was more likely that Mildred would sink the boat than find the treasure, but she might just do it.

Well, thought Ethel, there's one sure-fire way to make sure she doesn't get the chance.

Mildred decided to abandon Tabby's dinner for the night. She couldn't face another trip down the cliff, either by broomstick or on foot, so the best thing to do seemed to be to go to sleep and sneak out at the crack of dawn. She had completely forgotten the story she had made up to Ethel about the boat trip to Cat's Head Rock. In fact, she had completely forgotten Ethel until she saw her come back into the dormitory with an 'I-know-something-you-don't-know' look all over her face.

Ethel had obviously been out again. Her hair was windswept and she was wearing her cloak, which she folded neatly on top of her suitcase before she came and stood at the foot of Mildred's mat.

'I wouldn't bother going on any trip if I were you,' she announced.

'What trip?' asked Mildred, con-
fused for a moment. 'Oh yes! The trip
to the rock. Yes – well, as I told you, I
decided against it. *You* know best
about these things, Ethel.'

'Just in case you change your mind,'
said Ethel darkly, 'why don't you take
a look out of the window.'

Mildred sprang to her feet and
peered out into the darkening night.

Far below, in the deep shadow of the cove, she could just make out the shape of the boat, no longer attached to the breakwater, making its way steadily out into the open sea.

'Ethel you – you –' Words failed Mildred as she ran to the door, pulling on her cardigan and cloak over her pyjamas. 'Why can't you ever leave anything alone?'

'Don't make such a fuss, Mildred!' said Ethel feeling a little embarrassed, as half the class was now propped up in their beds, listening. 'It's only a boat for goodness' sake.'

Only a boat! thought Mildred, as she raced through the stone corridors and began the descent down the rickety steps. It says a lot for her desperation to rescue Tabby, that she didn't stop to remember that she was afraid of the dark.

CHAPTER EIGHTEEN

tanding at the edge of the waves with her eyes as wide open as possible, Mildred tried to gauge how far the boat had progressed. It certainly seemed a long way away, and the growing breeze was a little alarming, ruffling white crests on to the edge of the waves. Fortunately, a perfect full moon was rising above the horizon, casting a strong enough light to make Mildred less desperate about being out alone in the dark. There seemed to be nothing she could do. She couldn't swim at all, not even the doggie-paddle. If only she had a broomstick.

Suddenly, there was a loud miaow from the cave. Mildred's heart leapt – first in fright, then for joy as she thought that Tabby must have somehow got off the boat and be sheltering in the cave.

'Tabby!' she called as she ran to peer into the darkness, but the cat which pattered out to rub itself against her ankles was not a tabby, but a beautiful, sleek, black one. Mildred noticed the broomstick leaning against the wall just inside the cave as she bent down and picked up the cat.

'Now who do *you* belong to?' asked Mildred. 'Hello? Is there anyone there?' she called into the dark corners of the cave.

The complete stillness of the cave was her reply. The cat was now entwining itself round the broomstick, which Mildred caught as it toppled over sideways.

'*I* know!' she exclaimed, as an idea struck her. 'Here's your rescuer, Tabby! It won't take a minute on this to zoom out to the boat and bring you back! Perhaps I could even bring back the boat and no one would be any the wiser.'

She did wonder who the broomstick and cat belonged to, but of course there was no reason to suppose that they were Miss Hardbroom's. Poor Mildred would have been even more terrified if she had known that she was setting out on Miss Hardbroom's best broomstick and that Miss Hardbroom herself was in the boat.

'Drat that Ethel!' she muttered as she pulled her cape around her shoulders. 'I know she didn't realize about Tabby, but it's still an awful thing to do to unmoor a boat and just shove it out to sea – and I just *know* I'm bound to get the blame if it isn't back at the breakwater by the morning. You stay here in this nice warm cave, little cat – I won't be long.'

She pushed the cat firmly back into
the cave as, to Mildred's surprise, it
tried to jump on to the back of the
broomstick, which was hovering patiently in mid-air as she had commanded it.

'Off we go then!' said Mildred,
climbing on and giving the stick a
brisk tap, and they set off up the
beach, skimming the waves like a
hovercraft.

Unfortunately Mildred had forgotten Miss Hardbroom's warning about
the broomstick not working if it was

damp, and instead of rising above the water she ploughed straight into it.

There was enough air trapped under Mildred's cloak to hold her up

amid the waves, giving her time to remember how Ethel had come to grief during the broomstick water-skiing because she didn't hold it high above the water. It was very hard not to panic, but Mildred managed to tread water well enough to stop herself sinking.

She grabbed the broomstick and held it as far up in the air as she could.

'Fly! *Please* fly!' she gasped. 'Off we go, *nice* broom, *beautiful* broom. *Please*.'

Perhaps it was the flattery that did

it, despite the broomstick being completely waterlogged. Very jerkily it
rose above the waves pulling Mildred
out of the sea, water cascading from
her clothes.

'Stop!' Mildred shouted rather suddenly as she realized that they were now ten feet in the air and rising. It had been difficult to tell how far they had risen because the moon had disappeared completely behind a sinister-looking black cloud, and the night was suddenly very dark.

Mildred could hardly believe that she had got into quite such a dreadful situation. Hanging by both arms from a broomstick is extremely difficult, even when your clothes are not twice as heavy with water. Mildred realized that there was only a limited amount of time that she could hold on, so she had only one hope and that was to find the boat and literally drop into it.

From her vantage point in mid-air she frantically peered all around into the pitch dark and tried to see where it was.

To her great surprise, the broomstick

suddenly gave a little twitch and set off in a most determined manner, as if it really knew where it was going. In fact, it *did* know where it was going. Magic broomsticks are very curious things. If they are owned by one person for a very long time (and Miss Hardbroom had kept this particular one for twenty-five years), they develop a strange kind of intuition about their owners. In the same way that a dog will stand at the front door and wag its tail when its master is getting off a bus at the end of the street, a broomstick can sometimes sense that its owner is nearby, and if the owner is in trouble, the sense is even more acute.

The broomstick flew on grimly until it stopped, just as suddenly, and hovered. Mildred felt desperate.

'Go on, broom!' she said. 'You were doing really well.'

But the broomstick didn't budge. Mildred's arms and fingers were almost numb with cold and pain from hanging on. She began to cry as she imagined the horror of being alone, unable to swim in the darkest of dark nights. It really was all her worst fears come true. Slowly her fingers loosened their grip; she let go completely and fell through the black night air towards the waiting sea.

CHAPTER NINETEEN

Instead of plunging into the soft, cold waves that she was expecting, Mildred landed with a jarring thud, half on something very hard, and half on something firm, but soft. She felt around and realized, partly from the rocking motion and partly from the feel of the planks, that it was a boat. She couldn't believe her luck when a loud miaowing began a few yards to her left.

'It's Tabby!' she gasped, feeling completely hysterical with relief. Fortunately, she remembered the broomstick, although now it had found its owner, it would have hovered patiently above the boat till someone came to the rescue.

'Down, broom!' called Mildred. 'Down here and rest!'

As it landed neatly next to her, Mildred flung her arms around it and gave it a hug.

'You brilliant, wonderful, *magic* broom!' she said. 'Thanks a million, billion, trillion!' But the broomstick just stayed stiffly in her arms, like any old broom you might have found in a backyard somewhere, and when she let it go it clattered to the deck, waiting for its next command. They're curious things, broomsticks.

Mildred got up to feel her way to the cabin and tripped over the soft

thing she had half landed on. She put
out her arms to try to ascertain what
it was, and was appalled when her
fingers closed around a cold, bony
hand. Mildred leapt back in horror,

wondering if perhaps she was having
some awful nightmare that might go
away if only she could wake up.

With marvellous timing, the moon
reappeared from the scudding clouds
for a brief moment and revealed various things to the petrified young witch.
The first was the astonishing sight of
Miss Hardbroom, apparently fast
asleep on the floor of the boat. The

second was dear old Tabby, still trying to scrabble his way out of the impossibly small opening in the window, and the third was the terrifying sight of Cat's Head Rock, looming like a gigantic sea monster only a few feet away.

The moon hung like a spotlight, as if some helpful person had decided to give Mildred a few clues, then, just as suddenly, the clouds closed over and it was dark again, though not as utterly dark as before. The clouds were not quite so dense this time and Mildred could still see the rock, as well as Miss Hardbroom stretched out at her feet.

Mildred groped her way to the prow of the boat and hauled in the long rope that had been untied and left trailing in the sea. There was only one thing to do. In the few seconds that the moon had floodlit the scene, Mildred had noticed that the rock was full of jagged promontories and crevices. If she could somehow wedge the boat into a crevice and tie it to a projecting piece of rock, they could stay there until daylight. Perhaps by then Miss Hardbroom might be awake and full of bright ideas.

However, right now the wind was getting stronger by the minute and the waves higher, so Mildred had to think fast. In fact, it was amazing how sensibly she behaved on this occasion, bearing in mind how ghastly everything seemed and how scatterbrained she was most of the time.

'Come on, broom,' she said. 'The rescue isn't over yet.'

She tied the rope as securely as possible on to the back of the broomstick, then held the broomstick up as high as possible.

'Off you go, broom!' she commanded. 'Straight above the rock! Now! Fast as you can!'

The broom shot away like a missile,

towing the boat along behind it with surprising ease.

'Stop now!' called Mildred desperately, a little too late, as the boat slammed into the rock, wedging itself perfectly into a boat-shaped crevice.

She was thrown several feet down the boat, head first into the cabin door, where she very nearly joined Miss Hardbroom unconscious on the floor.

Mildred staggered to her feet and hauled the broomstick back into the boat. She untied the rope and retied it several times around a large barnacled

piece of rock, just in case the boat relaunched itself. In fact, it was quite a sheltered crevice, the wind being in the opposite direction and blowing the waves away from them.

Mildred opened the cabin door so

that she could perhaps drag Miss Hardbroom inside, out of the cold, but the
formidable form-mistress was too
heavy to move, so Mildred took off
her sodden cloak, wrung it out, and
draped it over Miss Hardbroom to
keep out the wind. She sat hunched
up next to her teacher, rubbing the
long, bony hands in a useless attempt
to warm them up.

Tabby escaped at last through the open door and wrapped himself around Mildred's shoulders. Mildred

found him wonderfully warm and dry in the middle of all the wet clothes and breaking waves. She suddenly realized that Tabby could help to keep Miss Hardbroom warm, so she draped him around Miss Hardbroom's neck and told him to stay there.

She was so tired that she couldn't think any more, so she leaned half against the cabin and half against Miss Hardbroom to help with keeping her warm, and closed her eyes, hoping that perhaps it really *was* a nightmare and any minute now the rising bell would clang through the dormitory and wake her up.

CHAPTER TWENTY

Mildred awoke to the sound of her name being shouted very loudly by several voices. For a moment she thought she was on her mat at the castle, where she had woken up so stiff and aching from the draught at the window. However, this stiffness was a hundred times worse and her eyes felt puffy as she prized them open and looked around at the extraordinary sight. Miss Hardbroom was still in exactly the same position on the floor

of the boat, Tabby was asleep, purring, on Mildred's lap, the broomstick
was lying across the two bench seats,
and all around was a cloudless blue
sky and a perfectly calm, innocent-
looking sea. Mildred's clothes were so
thoroughly wet that she couldn't
imagine ever feeling warm again.

'Mildred! Mildred Hubble!' called
a voice from the other side of the rock.

'Over here!' croaked Mildred. 'I'm on the other side; over here!'

To Mildred's eternal delight, Maud and Enid zoomed into sight on their broomsticks and landed on the rock just above the boat. They couldn't believe their eyes when they saw Miss Hardbroom.

'Gosh, Mil!' said Maud. 'I know you and Miss Hardbroom don't quite see eye to eye about things, but what on earth's happened?'

'*I* don't know,' said Mildred. 'I came to rescue Tabby, that's all, and Miss Hardbroom was in the boat when I found it. She's still breathing, but she's been unconscious for ages. We must get her back.'

'What's Tabby doing here?' asked Enid. 'He's supposed to be at the Academy!'

'Oh I'll explain all that later,' said Mildred. 'I can't tell you how pleased I am to see you. It was really grim last night. I didn't think I'd make it.'

'Everyone's out looking for you,' explained Maud. 'Poor Miss Cackle's nearly gone out of her mind with worry, although when she discovered that Miss Hardbroom was missing, she thought perhaps you might be all right together. Anyway, this morning we all broke up into groups and set off to find you.'

'*I* know,' said Mildred. 'Let's tie the rope on to one of the broomsticks and let it fly us home. This one —' she patted Miss Hardbroom's recumbent broomstick – 'was quite fantastic last night. I found it in the cave on the beach and it seemed to *know* where the boat was.'

'That's because it's Miss Hardbroom's broomstick, silly!' said Maud.

'Miss Cackle found her cat, Morgana, on the beach, so she must have left her broomstick in the cave . . . I say, Mil – Ethel must be having kittens. I mean, we all *heard* her say she'd let the boat out. Do you think she knew that Miss Hardbroom was in it?'

'Perhaps she knocked her out and pushed the boat out on purpose!' exclaimed Enid.

'Even Ethel's not *that* bad,' said Mildred. 'No, she pushed the boat out because I'd told her that I was taking it out to get the supposed treasure off this rock. I wasn't *really*. I was only going down the steps to feed Tab – I'd hidden him in the boat for the holiday. I made up the story to put Ethel off the scent. I suppose she couldn't bear the thought of me *possibly* finding the treasure. She didn't know about Tabby being on the boat and probably not about Miss Hardbroom either. She really *did* think it was just a boat. Anyway, let's get H.B. back to the castle as fast as possible. It can't be doing her any good lying here in those damp clothes. Ethel is an idiot – fancy doing all that just in case I upstaged her by finding some mythical treasure chest!'

Mildred began untying the rope from the projecting piece of rock and, as she did so, she noticed that the rock was a rather odd shape, not jagged or pointed, but with neat, sheared-off sides almost hidden beneath barnacles and fronds of seaweed. She scraped at the seaweed and a large, unmistakable hinge appeared. More scraping

revealed a stout wooden plank and another and another.

'It's a chest!' gasped Mildred. 'Look! It really is a chest!'

'We'll never get it free from the rock,' said Enid. 'It's practically grown into it, look.'

'We could see if one of the broomsticks could pull it free,' said Mildred. 'Miss Hardbroom's broomstick seems to be as strong as an ox.'

'Let's try!' said Maud.

So they untied the boat end of the rope and tied it firmly on to Miss Hardbroom's broomstick.

'Pull, broom!' said Mildred. 'Pull as hard as you can and stop when I tell you.'

The broomstick set off very fast,
several feet above the water, until the
rope was taut and the chest was
wrenched with a sudden ripping of
barnacles, years of sea and salt and
swollen wood, clean out of the rock-
face, where it fell conveniently into
the boat, narrowly missing Miss Hardbroom by a few inches.

'Stop!' yelled Mildred. The broom was still pulling as firmly as possible, nearly turning the boat on its side. 'Down and rest.'

'Shall we try to open it?' asked Maud.

'It's very rusty,' said Enid. 'I think we'll need a crowbar.'

'Or dynamite!' suggested Mildred.

'No, first and foremost we *must* get H.B. back to the castle. Let's tie the rope on to the front of the boat again and see if H.B.'s broomstick can get us home. Perhaps you can both fly alongside to make the boat lighter.'

'You and Tab can ride on the back of my broom if you like,' said Maud. 'Then there'd just be H.B. and the chest for it to pull.'

'Good idea,' said Mildred.

'And we ought to both take off our capes and cover H.B. with them,' said Enid. 'She must be half frozen. I don't know why we didn't think of it before.'

Maud and Enid both took off their capes. Maud laid hers gently over their form-mistress and Enid rolled hers up to make a pillow. Tabby, who had heard the conversation about taking him on Maud's broomstick, made a dive for the cabin and refused to come out.

'Never mind,' said Mildred, scrambling on to the back of Maud's broom, which was hovering patiently with Maud already on it. 'He doesn't weigh much; he might as well stay on board.'

Miss Cackle was on the beach with various members of Form Two, who had come to report after making trips to search for Mildred and Miss Hardbroom.

'Look over there, girls!' exclaimed Miss Cackle. 'Isn't that a boat in the distance with some of our girls flying above it?'

Everyone craned their necks and screwed up their eyes against the sun to get a clearer view, and as the boat came nearer they could see Mildred on the back of Maud's broom, Enid next to Maud, and the spare broomstick pulling the boat along. They all let out a rousing cheer of delight.

'Mildred Hubble!' called Miss Cackle, not sure whether to be thrilled or angry. 'Come here at once and explain where on *earth* you have been, worrying us all senseless.'

The boat coasted alongside the breakwater, expertly steered by the broomstick under Mildred's orders. Everyone ran to help and stopped in their tracks when they saw Miss Hardbroom lying in the boat wrapped in the cloaks. Tabby chose this moment to come miaowing out of the cabin and jump on to the chest.

Miss Cackle stood and stared in complete bewilderment. So did all the other members of Form Two.

'Oh dear,' said Mildred. 'This is all going to be very difficult to explain.'

CHAPTER TWENTY-ONE

The magician arrived back early when he received word of Miss Hardbroom's accident. He materialized in a swirl of brilliant-coloured smoke in the middle of the courtyard, dusted himself down and strode indoors, watched from the windows of their dormitory by the members of Form Two.

Mildred, Maud and Enid climbed down from the window and sat in a row on Mildred's mat, each of them cuddling their cat.

'At least I've got Tabby back for the day,' said Mildred gloomily. 'Though they're bound to be absolutely *raving* after last night. Goodness knows what'll happen.'

Ethel looked very nervous too, which was most unusual for her.

'If any of you say *anything* about me pushing the boat out,' said Ethel, 'I'll – I'll –'

'Oh it's all right, bossy boots,' said Maud. 'No one's going to sneak on you. *You're* the sneak around here, remember.'

Maud could be quite withering when she wanted to.

Suddenly, there was a knock on the door. They all leaped to their feet and stood by their assorted beds, thinking that it must be Miss Cackle, as Miss Hardbroom was in bed tucked up with a hot-water bottle, a bandaged head and a pile of warm blankets.

But it wasn't Miss Cackle. It was the magician and, to everyone's surprise, he was smiling and looking just as genial as the day they had arrived.

'Mildred, my dear,' he said. 'Come

with me.' He led Mildred through the
maze of passages to Miss Hardbroom's
room where, to Mildred's relief min-
gled with terror, Miss Hardbroom was
wide awake, sitting propped up in bed
with a huge white bandage around

her head. Miss Cackle was perched on
a chair on the other side of the bed.
Miss Cackle smiled in welcome, but
Miss Hardbroom looked grim.

'Come in, Mildred,' said Miss Cackle. 'You'll be relieved to hear that Miss Hardbroom is perfectly all right after her terrible ordeal in the boat. I'm afraid she'll have to spend the rest of the holiday in bed after such a nasty knock on the head, but I'm sure you girls will be able to cope for a few days away from the firm guidance of your form-mistress.'

'Oh yes, Miss Cackle!' agreed Mildred, sounding a little too eager.

Miss Hardbroom shot a menacing glance in her direction.

'I mean –' contrived Mildred hastily – 'of course we'll soldier on and do our *best*, but it will all be much more difficult without Miss Hardbroom at the helm.'

'All right, Mildred,' muttered Miss Hardbroom. 'There's no need to overdo it.'

'Now then, Mildred,' said Miss

Cackle, rising from her chair and pushing her glasses on top of her head. 'About yesterday's little escapade.'

Oh dear, thought Mildred. Here we go.

'If you hadn't disobeyed orders and brought that dreadful cat, which should have been in the kitchen catching mice,' said Miss Cackle, looking serious, 'Miss Hardbroom would not have climbed into the boat to investigate when she saw it at the window, thereby avoiding the fall which knocked her out.'

'No, Miss Cackle,' agreed Mildred, looking at the floor.

'However,' continued Miss Cackle, 'neither would you have discovered the chest which you brought back from the rock, which *is* after all the very same treasure chest described to you by the magician in the folk-tale about the shipwrecked sailor. Yes, Mildred, the chest is packed with gold coins and the most gorgeous jewellery.'

Mildred didn't know how to react. She looked around the room, first at Miss Cackle, who was looking thrilled and excited, then at the magician, who was smiling at her with a vaguely fond expression, and finally at Miss Hard-broom, who looked as if she would like to expel her worst pupil on the spot.

'What will happen to Tabby?' she asked.

The magician stepped forward and put an arm around Mildred's shoulders.

'You must be so proud of this child, Miss Cackle,' he said. 'And especially you, Miss Hardbroom, after she saved your life. Most girls would want to know if they could have the treasure, but not *this* girl. The only thing she wants in the world is her little cat, and I can't see any reason why she shouldn't have it, can you?'

'Well, I really don't think –' began Miss Hardbroom, but the magician cut across her.

'I mean to say, Miss Hardbroom, the cat actually wrapped itself around your neck to keep you warm all night. It's the least reward we can give to Mildred to let her keep her little life-saver.'

'If you think so, your Honour,' said Miss Hardbroom, trying to look gracious.

'And as for the treasure,' said the magician, 'there's enough to do all the repairs to the castle here *and* to give you a substantial amount for Miss Cackle's Academy.'

'Oh, Mr Rowan-Webb!' exclaimed Miss Cackle. 'How simply wonderful. I've been wondering how we were going to pay for the new roof on the west wing – perhaps there'll even be enough left for a swimming-pool!'

'Could I go and tell Tabby the good news?' asked Mildred, anxious to leave the room before any more questions were asked.

'Of course,' said Miss Cackle.

'I'll escort you back to your dormitory,' said the magician.

Just outside the dormitory door, the magician handed a small package to Mildred.

'This is a little present from the treasure chest,' he said. 'I thought you ought to have a memento, and it seemed rather appropriate. I still haven't forgotten how you rescued *me* last year. Enjoy the rest of your stay, my dear. It's bound to be a little easier with your form-mistress recovering in her room.'

The dormitory was empty, except for the cats. Everyone had been called to the hall for a late breakfast. Mildred could hardly wait to join them and share the wonderful news about Miss Hardbroom being out of action for the rest of the holiday. Before she left the room, she curled up for a quick hug of Tabby and to find out what was in the magician's package.

It was a gold chain with a delightful pendant composed of two golden frogs, one with emeralds for eyes, the other with rubies. They were sitting solemnly facing each other, shaking hands. Mildred put it on and slipped it out of sight beneath her shirt as a secret good-luck charm, where she kept it for ever, even when she grew up. Certainly that day, as she raced down the sunlit stairs to find her friends and tell them all her news, she felt like the luckiest girl in the world instead of the worst witch in the school.

READ MORE IN PUFFIN

For children of all ages, Puffin represents quality and variety – the very best in publishing today around the world.

For complete information about books available from Puffin – and Penguin – and how to order them, contact us at the appropriate address below. Please note that for copyright reasons the selection of books varies from country to country.

On the worldwide web: www.puffin.co.uk

In the United Kingdom: Please write to *Dept. EP, Penguin Books Ltd, Bath Road, Harmondsworth, West Drayton, Middlesex UB7 0DA*

In the United States: Please write to *Consumer Sales, Penguin USA, P.O. Box 999, Dept. 17109, Bergenfield, New Jersey 07621-0120*. VISA and MasterCard holders call 1-800-253-6476 to order Penguin titles

In Canada: Please write to *Penguin Books Canada Ltd, 10 Alcorn Avenue, Suite 300, Toronto, Ontario M4V 3B2*

In Australia: Please write to *Penguin Books Australia Ltd, P.O. Box 257, Ringwood, Victoria 3134*

In New Zealand: Please write to *Penguin Books (NZ) Ltd, Private Bag 102902, North Shore Mail Centre, Auckland 10*

In India: Please write to *Penguin Books India Pvt Ltd, 706 Eros Apartments, 56 Nehru Place, New Delhi 110 019*

In the Netherlands: Please write to *Penguin Books Netherlands bv, Postbus 3507, NL-1001 AH Amsterdam*

In Germany: Please write to *Penguin Books Deutschland GmbH, Metzlerstrasse 26, 60594 Frankfurt am Main*

In Spain: Please write to *Penguin Books S. A., Bravo Murillo 19, 1° B, 28015 Madrid*

In Italy: Please write to *Penguin Italia s.r.l., Via Felice Casati 20, I-20124 Milano*

In France: Please write to *Penguin France S. A., 17 rue Lejeune, F-31000 Toulouse*

In Japan: Please write to *Penguin Books Japan, Ishikiribashi Building, 2-5-4, Suido, Bunkyo-ku, Tokyo 112*

In South Africa: Please write to *Longman Penguin Southern Africa (Pty) Ltd, Private Bag X08, Bertsham 2013*